W9-BRS-655

# THE PRINCESS AND THE UNICORN

A.M. Luzzader

Illustrated by Anna M. Clark

Published by Knowledge Forest Press
P.O. Box 6331
Logan, UT 84341

Ebook ISBN-13: 978-1-949078-43-5
Paperback ISBN-13: 978-1-949078-42-8

Cover design by Sleepy Fox Studio, www.sleepyfoxstudio.net

Editing by Chadd VanZanten

Interior illustrations by Anna M. Clark, annamclarkart.com

*For Juniper, sweet, smart, and cute!—A.M.L.*

*For my strong niece, Lily. —A.M.C.*

*The real-life Princess Olivia and Princess Juniper*

## CONTENTS

## Chapter One

### IN WILDFLOWER KINGDOM

In a faraway place, in a faraway time, there once was a land called Wildflower Kingdom. It was called Wildflower Kingdom because, yes, there bloomed many kinds of beautiful wildflowers. Bright yellow sunflowers, red poppies, purple clover, blue colored bluebells, and others grew all around the kingdom.

There were wild violets and buttercups, too. All through the spring and summer, the hillsides and meadows of the kingdom bloomed with color.

Wildflower Kingdom was a very pretty place. For example, the sunrises in the kingdom were stunning. In fact, they almost named the kingdom "Sunrise Kingdom," but that name was already taken by some other kingdom. Also, the moon shone big and bright each night, and so they wanted to name the place "Moonbeam Kingdom," but that name was taken, too. And so they decided to name the kingdom after the wildflowers. Someone checked with all the other kingdoms, and the name "Wildflower Kingdom" was still available.

And so there were amazing wildflowers, sunrises, and night skies, but Wildflower Kingdom was beautiful for other reasons. During the day, the bright blue skies were dotted with cute, fluffy little clouds. Sparkling streams with wondrous waterfalls flowed through the grand hills and mountains. And growing with the wildflowers of violet, yellow, and pink, there was plenty of lush, wild grass.

It was good that lots of green grass grew there, because Wildflower Kingdom was magical. As you may already know, most magical kingdoms are home to unicorns. Many unicorns lived in Wildflower Kingdom, and they feasted on the delicious green grass.

Not all magical kingdoms had dragons, but Wildflower Kingdom had one. It had enormous fangs and was covered in hard scales. He could usually be found coiled up in a cave in one of the high, rocky cliffs. The dragon's name was Patrick, and although some dragons are cruel and dangerous, this one wasn't. In fact, Patrick was a very nice dragon who helped to keep watch over Wildflower Kingdom.

Wildflower Kingdom had a queen and king. Queen Jennifer of Wildflower Kingdom was kind and intelligent. She had beautiful green eyes and a warm smile. King Andrew was tall and brave. He had sharp blue eyes and a thick black beard. The king and queen were always very busy making sure that everyone in the kingdom was happy and healthy.

Queen Jennifer
King Andrew
Princess Olivia
Princess Juniper

Queen Jennifer and King Andrew had two daughters, Olivia and Juniper. Princess Olivia was eight years old. She had green eyes and a sweet smile. She loved foxes and riding her bike. Princess Juniper was six years old. She had big blue eyes and often wore her hair in pigtails. She loved puppies and was very good at climbing trees.

Juniper and Olivia lived with Queen Jennifer and King Andrew in Wildflower Castle. It was a mighty castle with white towers and colorful banners. The castle sat on a hill surrounded by meadows of green grass and colorful flowers.

Many other people lived in Wildflower Castle. There was a wizard who did magic and a school teacher who taught lessons. There was also a chef, a baker, and a shoemaker. Many others lived in the castle, and each did their part to make Wildflower Castle a nice place. Olivia and Juniper were the only children who lived there, and so they often played together.

Sometimes the princesses pretended to be animals. Princess Olivia might pretend to be a fox.

"Yip, yip, yip!" she would say as she scampered around.

Princess Juniper would pretend to be a puppy.

"Woof, woof!" she would say as she chased her sister.

Other times, Princess Olivia and Princess Juniper pretended that they were animal doctors helping sick or injured unicorns, cats, or dogs. They also enjoy playing with their dolls, jumping rope, and exploring the forest around Wildflower Castle.

Most of all, Princess Juniper and Princess Olivia enjoyed riding unicorns. You probably wanted to hear more about the unicorns, so we'll discuss them now. Unicorns are very rare, meaning they're hard to find. However, in Wildflower Kingdom, there were many, many unicorns.

Unicorns are similar to horses, but they have fancy horns on their foreheads. The horns of unicorns are usually spiraled and very colorful. Some unicorns have white bodies with colorful tails and manes, but unicorns can be almost any color you can think of.

Princess Olivia and Princess Juniper had named their favorite unicorns. The one with the white coat and pink mane and tail they named Cupcake, because she reminded them of a cupcake with pink frosting. There was another unicorn with a pink coat and whose tail and mane were red, yellow, and orange. They named her Diva, because she was always very dramatic. Snowflake was named for her silver coat and snowy white mane and tail. Another of the unicorns had a black coat, and his mane and tail were colored a glittery purple. He was called Sparkles.

There were many other unicorns, and the princesses gave them names like Blossom, Buttercup, Treasure, and Honey, but their favorites were Cupcake, Diva, Snowflake, and Sparkles.

The unicorns of Wildflower Kingdom loved to give rides to people. They thought it was great fun to gallop through the grass or leap over hedges with someone riding on their backs. The unicorns of Wildflower Kingdom loved humans and wanted to spend as much time with them as possible. This was great for the two princesses, because riding unicorns happened to be their favorite thing to do.

The princesses weren't allowed to ride the unicorns by themselves. A grown-up had to be with them to make sure they didn't fall out of the saddle or get lost while riding. Usually, Juniper and Olivia would go unicorn riding with their mom or dad. Sometimes it was King Andrew and Princess Juniper riding together on Sparkles, with Juniper riding at the front of the saddle and her father seated behind to hold her steady. Other times it was Queen Jennifer with Princess Olivia riding together on Cupcake, with Olivia riding up front and her mother behind her. At other times they all went riding together. But always, each princess had an adult riding with her for safety.

Then, one day, something changed in Wildflower Kingdom. It was something that made one of the sisters glad and the other sister mad.

## Chapter Two

### BIG ENOUGH

King Andrew, Queen Jennifer, Princess Juniper, and her older sister, Princess Olivia, went outside that morning to decide which unicorns to ride. On the air was the sweet smell of wild lilacs, and the sun beamed through the cute, fluffy little clouds.

"Mom," said Olivia, "Let's ride Honey today! She hasn't been out for a good run in a while."

"Good idea," said Queen Jennifer.

"Dad," said Juniper, "I want to ride on Snowflake. He's very good at jumping over the stream."

The girls always approached the unicorns carefully so that they didn't startle them. The unicorns neighed happily when they saw the family.

Then Queen Jennifer said something surprising. "Olivia," said the queen. "You've grown so tall and strong, I think you're big enough now to ride a unicorn by yourself."

"Yes," added King Andrew, nodding. "It's time for you to ride on your own, Olivia."

That's when Olivia noticed that her parents had brought out three saddles instead of only two. There was a saddle for King Andrew and Juniper, one for Queen Jennifer, and one for Olivia by herself. Olivia's eyes grew wide and her mouth opened.

"Really?" said Olivia. "That's wonderful!"

"Have you noticed how tall you've grown?" said King Andrew.

Olivia looked down at her legs and arms. "I guess I didn't notice."

"It happens slowly, doesn't it?" said Queen Jennifer.

King Andrew looked around at the unicorns. "Why don't you ride Cupcake. She trots gently and would be good for a beginner."

Cupcake trotted over, and King Andrew helped Olivia fasten the saddle onto the unicorn's back and around its middle. Then Olivia climbed into the saddle. She put her feet into the stirrups and took the reins. Cupcake whinnied and trotted in a circle, happy to carry Olivia by herself.

"You're a natural," said Queen Jennifer.

King Andrew clapped merrily and smiled.

Olivia laughed and shouted with glee.

But Juniper wasn't happy.

In fact, Juniper was quite upset.

"What about me?" she demanded. "Can I ride by myself, too?"

King Andrew knelt next to Juniper so he could look her in the eye. "Yes, Juniper," he said, "you *can* ride a unicorn by yourself, but not just yet. You're still a wee bit small. But don't worry. You and your sister are growing up very quickly. You'll be big and tall enough to ride by yourself very soon."

"I don't want to wait," said Juniper with a frown. "I want to ride by myself now."

"Come ride with me," said Queen Jennifer. "You can pick any unicorn you want."

"But it's not fair," said Juniper. "If Olivia gets to ride a unicorn by herself, then I should get to as well."

"Olivia is older," said Queen Jennifer.

"And she's bigger and taller," said King Andrew. "It's hard to control a unicorn when you can't reach the stirrups. And it's impossible to stay in the saddle. When you're a little stronger, and your legs are a little longer, you'll be able to get your feet into the stirrups and stay in the saddle all by yourself."

Juniper and her mom both got on Snowflake, but Juniper was cross. She folded her arms and wouldn't smile. Usually, Juniper loved riding unicorns with her mom or dad behind her in the saddle, but now it didn't seem like fun at all. Even though they rode all over Wildflower Kingdom–crossing through streams, leaping over fences, and stopping to admire the waterfalls–all Juniper could think about was riding by herself.

When they got back to the castle, King Andrew rode next to Olivia, and said, "Well, how was it?"

"Amazing!" cried Olivia with a big smile on her face. She trotted Cupcake around in another little circle. "I didn't think I could enjoy riding unicorns more than I already did, but I do! I love to ride by myself!"

Olivia didn't mean to make Juniper sad, but Juniper frowned even harder. As soon as King Andrew helped her down from Snowflake, Juniper stormed inside the castle without saying anything.

"Where are you going?" Queen Jennifer called.

"There's something I've got to do!" Juniper yelled without looking back.

King Andrew and Queen Jennifer looked at each other.

"She's up to something," said King Andrew.

"She always is," said Queen Jennifer.

# Chapter Three

## A PLAN IN PROGRESS

AFTER HELPING HER PARENTS BRUSH THE UNICORNS AND put away the harnesses and saddles, Olivia headed to her bedroom. She was surprised to find her little sister, Juniper, waiting for her outside her bedroom door.

"Olivia, I need your help," said Juniper.

"What is it?" asked Olivia.

Juniper opened her hands to reveal a measuring tape in one hand and a pencil and notepad in the other.

"Will you measure how tall I am?" Juniper asked.

"Why?" asked Olivia.

"Oh, you'll see," said Juniper.

"Is this about riding the unicorns?" Olivia asked.

"You can't grow tall enough to ride by yourself in one day. It takes a long time to grow."

"We'll see about that," whispered Juniper.

"What did you say?" asked Olivia.

"Uh, nothing," said Juniper. In truth, Juniper had a plan to grow taller right away. But she didn't tell Olivia. Instead, she said, "I'm just curious to know how tall I am."

Olivia shrugged her shoulders and told Juniper to stand against the wall. Then she stretched the measuring tape from Juniper's feet to the top of her head. Olivia wrote the measurement on the notepad and gave the page to Juniper.

"Here you go," said Olivia. "That's your height."

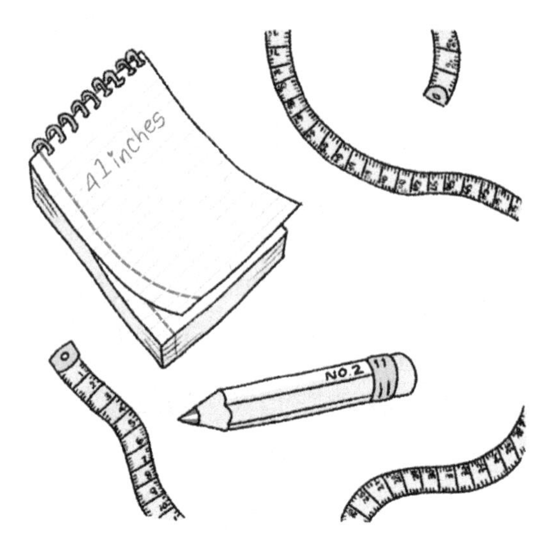

"Thank you," said Juniper. "Oh, and Olivia, do you want to ride unicorns later today?"

"You want to go again? Today? You didn't seem to enjoy it this morning," said Olivia.

"I'm sure I'll enjoy it later on today," said Juniper.

"Okay then," said Olivia. "Make sure you ask mom or dad."

"I will," said Juniper.

Juniper went to her bedroom and taped the slip of paper to her wall. Then she looked at the numbers.

"I'm pretty short right now," thought Juniper, "so growing tall should be easy! Now, it's time to get to work."

## Chapter Four

### LITTLE BY LITTLE

JUNIPER STARTED BY GOING TO THE PLAYGROUND IN THE yard outside her bedroom. There was a long slide, a swing set, and a kid-sized castle to play in. But Juniper went straight to the monkey bars. She climbed up toward the top, and she climbed rather like a monkey. Juniper was small and very light, and so she was very good at climbing. She also had no fear of heights. She loved to climb trees, castle walls, monkey bars, and almost anything else.

When she had reached to the top of the monkey bars, she hung down from the highest bar, swinging slightly.

Juniper felt her muscles stretching. She felt her arms stretching. Her back stretched, too. And her legs hung down beneath her.

"Yes," said Juniper with a smile. "I can feel myself getting taller already."

After a while, Juniper's muscles burned as gravity pulled her down. When she couldn't hold on any longer, Juniper let herself drop to the ground. She felt a little taller already, but she knew it was not enough to stay in the saddle and ride by herself. Not yet, anyhow. There was much more work to do.

And so Juniper did lots of stretches. She bent over and touched her toes. She lifted her arms high into the sky. And she bent as far backwards as she could. Again she felt her arms and legs getting longer. She twisted, reached, and stretched.

After that, Juniper got back onto the monkey bars and let herself hang down again. She looked around and saw the slide and the swing set and the little toy ride-on unicorn that sat on top of a big spring.

Juniper was getting hot and tired, and she thought about giving up and just playing in the playground, but she kept hanging and stretching. For one entire hour, Juniper hung down from the monkey bars and did her stretching exercises. Juniper believed that one hour was a very long time, and so she knew her plan was working.

When Juniper got too tired and thirsty to continue, she went back into the castle. Now that she was tall, she was careful to duck down a little so that she wouldn't bump her head on the top of the doorway. She stopped for a drink in the castle's kitchen, and next she fetched her notepad and measurement paper, a pencil, and the measuring tape. Then she returned to Olivia's room.

Olivia was lying on her bed reading a book. When

she didn't look up, Juniper cleared her throat.

"Oh, you again," said Olivia. "Are you ready to ride unicorns now? You could probably ride with dad this time if you wanted."

"Yes," said Juniper. "Yes, I am ready to ride unicorns now, but I won't be riding with Dad or anyone else."

"What do you mean?" asked Olivia, setting aside her book.

"Well," said Juniper, "I think if you use this measuring tape, you will see that I am much taller than I was earlier today."

Olivia scratched her head. "How could that be? We just measured you this morning."

"It's been an entire hour!" said Juniper. "Measure me!"

Olivia shrugged and got off her bed. "Stand against the wall," she said to Juniper. "Hold still."

Olivia unrolled the measuring tape. Juniper stretched her back and neck, trying to be as tall as possible. Olivia wrote down the measurement.

"Well?" Juniper asked.

"Actually," answered Olivia, "according to this, you've gotten a little shorter. I may have measured wrong the first time."

"What?" said Juniper, grabbing the paper from Olivia. "That can't be right!"

"Well, it is," said Olivia. "Didn't I tell you that you can't grow that much in just one day?"

"But I stretched!" cried Juniper. "I hung down from the monkey bars for one *entire* hour!"

Olivia went back to her bed and began reading her book again. Juniper picked up the measuring tape and went back to her own room.

"I thought for sure I was taller," Juniper grumbled to herself. "But if stretching doesn't work, what else could make me grow?"

Juniper sat on her bed to think about it, and that's when she got a new idea.

"I never notice myself growing," said Juniper, "which means that it must happen when I'm *asleep!* So, if I just get some extra sleep, I'll have extra growth, and then I'll be tall enough to ride a unicorn by myself!"

Juniper climbed into her covers and closed her eyes, but she couldn't fall asleep.

"This isn't my normal bedtime," she thought. "That's why I'm not sleepy. Oh, well. As long as my eyes are shut and I lie very still, the growing will happen and my plan will still work."

And so this is what Juniper did. She lay down on her bed. She kept her eyes closed. She didn't move–well, not very much. She had to scratch her nose once, but then she lay still again. This wasn't easy.

"This is almost harder than hanging from the monkey bars for so long," she thought.

Juniper's nose itched again but she didn't scratch it. She felt fidgety. She wanted a drink of water. She wanted to play outside. She wanted to read a book. She wanted to turn over or get up and have a snack. But Juniper knew she'd need to stay there a long time in order to grow big enough.

All she could think about was how much fun it would be to ride on Honey's back without any help.

Or Buttercup. Or Sparkle. Or any of the unicorns. She would soon ride them all by herself, and only she and the unicorn would decide where to go. No parents, no one else in the saddle. Juniper was daydreaming about this as she lay on her bed. Once she could ride by herself, maybe she'd teach the unicorns some new tricks, or maybe even dance moves. In Juniper's daydream, all the unicorns were begging her to ride them.

"Now, now," Juniper told them in her daydream. "You'll all get a turn. Just wait, and be patient, and I'll teach you all the new tricks!"

Suddenly, Juniper woke up!

She had been so still and quiet that she had fallen asleep. Feeling refreshed, she sat up and rubbed her eyes. She had no way to know how long she'd been asleep, but she guessed it had been another entire hour plus about fourteen minutes.

"Now I'm really tall!" she thought. "Now I know I'm big enough to ride alone!"

She got the measuring tape and raced back to Olivia's room. She poked her head in. Olivia was still reading the book.

"You again?" Olivia asked, looking over the top of her book.

"Wow, are you still reading that same book?" asked Juniper. "You must be a slow reader."

"What do you want this time?" asked Olivia. "Do you want to go riding again or not?"

"Yes," said Juniper, "but I wondered if you could measure me again. I'm taller now; I know I am. I've been lying in bed for another entire hour plus about fourteen minutes."

"An hour?" said Olivia. She laughed. "You were here ten minutes ago."

Had it really only been ten minutes? That wasn't enough time to grow taller. Even Juniper knew that. And so she thought up yet another plan to help her grow.

"Are you sure that was only ten minutes?" asked Juniper.

"I'm positive," said Olivia.

"Okay," said Juniper. "I've got another idea. Stay here."

"I was planning to," said Olivia, lifting her book again.

Juniper left Olivia's bedroom and ran to the kitchen. There she found the chef of the castle, Bertha Beets, preparing that evening's dinner. Miss

Beets was tall. She had curly blonde hair and a loud, happy voice.

"Excuse me, Miss Beets?" asked Juniper. "Could I please have some vegetables?"

"Vegetables?" cried Miss Beets. She was stirring a large pot of raspberry sauce. She tapped the spoon on the saucepan and set it down. "This is a big change!" she cried. "Usually, you ask me for candy or cookies. But if it's vegetables you are wanting, it's vegetables you will have."

She quickly prepared a little plate with fresh broccoli, carrots, and celery. "Here you are, my dear!" said Miss Beets in her loud, sing-song voice.

"Thank you," said Juniper.

Then Juniper took the plate to her bedroom and sat cross-legged on her bed while she munched on the vegetables. Yes, candy and cookies were her favorite, but they wouldn't help her to be tall or strong enough to ride a unicorn. No, her parents always said it was vegetables that helped children grow big and strong. She crunched the vegetables one at a time, trying to get all the nutrients. With the stretching, sleeping, and vegetables, Juniper was sure she'd now be tall enough. When she'd popped the last stick of celery into her mouth, she returned to Olivia's room.

Olivia sighed and put down her book. "Ready to measure again?" she asked.

"Yes, please," answered Juniper. "I ate some celery and carrots just now. And also quite a bit of broccoli."

Olivia was happy to help her little sister, but she knew Juniper could not grow even one tiny inch in a single day. Olivia knew that Juniper would not be any taller than she had been in the morning.

"Juniper, people don't grow taller in one day,"

Olivia told her sister. "It happens really slowly, over time. Didn't you hear what Mom said? You grow so slowly, you don't even notice it. I used to be your size, and I didn't notice that I was tall enough to ride by myself until Mom and Dad told me this morning."

Juniper stuck out her bottom lip. "Are you sure?"

"Yes," said Olivia. "And it's impossible to grow that quickly."

"Well, will you still measure me? Just in case?" Juniper asked.

Olivia sighed again and rolled off her bed. "I'm never going to finish this book," she mumbled.

"Thank you, sister," said Juniper, backing up to the wall and standing up tall again.

Olivia measured Juniper and they found that nothing had changed. Olivia said, "See? It doesn't matter what you do. You can't make yourself grow taller in one day."

Juniper tossed down the measuring tape and the notepad and the slips of paper.

"Fine!" Juniper huffed. She stormed out of the room. "Then I'll just have to find some *other* way to be taller!"

## Chapter Five

### SOME OTHER WAY

JUNIPER WASN'T READY TO GIVE UP. SHE HEADED BACK to the kitchen for another chat with Miss Beets, and when she returned to her room, she was carrying two empty green-bean cans and a roll of string.

Miss Beets didn't know what Juniper was up to, but she helped Juniper poke some holes in the cans so that Juniper could tie them onto her feet. Juniper sat down on her bedroom floor and wrapped the string through the cans and over her feet. Then she used a nearby chair to help her stand up again.

Success!

The cans stayed on her feet, and now Juniper was much, much taller!

"Unicorns, here I come," said Juniper with a big

grin on her face.

But then she tried to walk.

*Calunk.* That was one step.

*Calunk, calunk.* That was two steps, then three.

But then Juniper wobbled. Next, she wiggled. Then she actually *wibbled*, which she wasn't sure was even possible, but before she could think about it, she crashed to the ground.

It didn't hurt. She didn't fall very far. She had only been one green-bean can high. So, she tried again, and this time she took four steps.

*Calunk, calunk, calunk, calunk, calunk.*

Actually, that was five steps. But she fell down once again. She hadn't even reached her bedroom door.

Yes, tying cans to her feet did make her taller, but the plan wouldn't work if she couldn't walk straight. Juniper looked around her room–there had to be something else she could use to make herself bigger.

She spotted the big fluffy pillows on her bed. They might be less stiff and clumsy than green-bean cans. She tied them to her feet, but they squished down and didn't make her very much taller at all, and besides they were too wide and made her walk like a giant duck.

Juniper tried books. These were too heavy.

She tried toys. None of them were the same size, so they were more awkward than the cans.

There seemed to be nothing that could make Juniper taller while also allowing her to move about easily. Still, Juniper was determined to find something that would work. She left her bedroom and began searching the castle, looking for anything she could tie onto her feet to make her tall enough.

When she reached the library, Juniper had a flowerpot strapped to one foot and an alarm clock tied to the other. She clomped noisily into the room only to find her parents, King Andrew and Queen Jennifer. They might have asked Juniper what she was doing with those odd things tied onto her feet, but they were having a serious talk. They had worried looks on their faces.

"What's wrong?" Juniper asked.

"It's Sparkles," said Queen Jennifer. "He's very sick."

Sparkles was a very special unicorn because his coat was pure black, and he had a sparkling mane and tail of long, purple hair.

"What's wrong with him?" Juniper asked.

"Sparkles hasn't been eating," said King Andrew.

"He has a fever and just wants to lie down all the time."

"Oh no!" said Juniper. She could remember when she had been sick herself earlier in the year. It wasn't any fun.

"The doctor said Sparkles needs the root of a marshmallow plant to get better," said King Andrew.

"But we can't find any!" said Queen Jennifer. "It's a very rare plant, and if we can't find some soon, he won't get better."

For the first time that day, Juniper stopped thinking about herself and riding unicorns by herself. She was worried about Sparkles.

## Chapter Six

### WORRIED ABOUT SPARKLES

PRINCESS OLIVIA AND PRINCESS JUNIPER BOTH SAT cross-legged on Olivia's bed. They were talking about Sparkles.

"Maybe we can give him some soup," suggested Juniper.

"No, Mom said he won't eat *anything*," said Olivia. "And if he doesn't eat, he'll only get weaker."

"Maybe he just needs to sleep more," said Juniper.

Olivia shrugged. "Maybe, but it would help if we could get him the medicine from the marshmallow plant like the doctor said."

"We should go look for some," said Juniper. "Maybe we could find it ourselves."

"Mom and Dad said practically everyone in the castle is out looking for the marshmallow plant," said Olivia. "But it's such a rare plant, and the kingdom is so large, no one has found any. And the doctor said Sparkle should have the plant today, or he might get sicker."

Juniper frowned. "If only we had a fox," she said.

"A fox?" Olivia asked.

"When Paul the candlestick maker was here, he

had a pet fox who could find things by smell," said Juniper.

"What?" Olivia said.

"Yeah, the fox was named Sylvia. She was really good at finding things," said Juniper.

"Juniper, that's it! Paul lives in the village. We just need to go ask him if Sylvia can help us find some marshmallow plant," said Olivia.

"Hurry," said Juniper, "Let's go tell mom and dad!"

As soon as the princesses told King Andrew and Queen Jennifer about Paul's fox, Sylvia, they sent a messenger to find Paul and ask him for help.

A short while later, Paul and Sylvia came to Wildflower Castle. Sylvia was a beautiful fox, with orange fur on her back and white fur on her nose and stomach. Her long tail was fluffy and came to a black point at the tip. Sylvia was taken care of by Paul, who had found her one day injured in the forest. Paul was a big, jolly man with a beard that was almost the same color as Sylvia's orange fur.

"We'd be happy to help!" said Paul. "I've asked Sylvia to help and she says she can hunt out the plant for us."

"That's wonderful," said Queen Jennifer.

"I hope she can find some," said King Andrew. "We really must have it today."

"Olivia, you stay with Sparkles," said the Queen.

"Okay, I will," said Olivia.

The king and queen quickly gathered up some unicorns for the hunt.

"Can I come with you?" asked Juniper.

"It was your idea," said King Andrew. "So, yes, of course you can come along!"

King Andrew helped Juniper to join him on Diva, the unicorn with the red, yellow, and orange colored mane and tail. Juniper sighed and frowned. She wanted to be riding a unicorn by herself, but riding with her dad was better than being left behind.

Paul rode on a unicorn named Honey, and Queen Jennifer rode on a unicorn named Treasure.

When they were all ready, Paul turned to Sylvia. "Okay, Sylvia, find us some marshmallow plant," he said.

The fox lifted her head and sniffed the air. She paced this way and that, putting her nose into the air to catch the scent. Then, all at once, she took off running.

## Chapter Seven

### THE DISCOVERY

SYLVIA THE FOX BOUNDED THROUGH THE GREEN FIELDS of Wildflower Kingdom, splashed through the Cubby River, and ran swiftly through the valley. They followed Sylvia for most of the day. Every now and then, Sylvia would stop and sniff the breeze and then hurry onward.

Close behind Sylvia, the king, queen, and Juniper, along with Paul the candlestick maker, rode their unicorns. Princess Juniper sat on the saddle with her father, crossing her fingers for luck and hoping that Sylvia the fox would be able to locate the marsh-mallow plant. But the sun was beginning to set, casting colors of pink, orange, and purple across the sky. If Sylvia couldn't find the plant soon, it would be too dark to continue searching.

Sylvia suddenly stopped running. Then she lifted her front paw and pointed her long nose toward a line of rocky hills off in the distance.

"We must be close," said Paul. "Keep following Sylvia, but don't follow too closely, or she might lose the scent." Sylvia went forward, stopping often to smell the air. She led them to the hills. They were craggy and uneven, with many cliffs and rocky outcroppings. Sylvia pointed at the cliffs.

Everyone got down from their unicorns and walked up to the steep and rocky hillside. Sylvia whimpered and pointed her nose at one very tall cliff. They all looked up.

"She's pointing way up there," said Paul, "to that rocky crack high up on the cliff."

"The doctor said the marshmallow plant is often found high up in rocky areas," said Queen Jennifer.

"Let's climb up and see," said King Andrew. He took off his cloak, grabbed onto the rocks, and began to climb. The rocks were sharp and some of them were loose. King Andrew was a large man, and it wasn't easy for him to climb so high and steep. The rocks beneath his boots came loose, and he slid down.

"Let me try," said Paul. "The marshmallow plant must be up there somewhere."

But Paul was a large man, too, and he struggled to climb only a little way up the cliff face. Loose rocks and pebbles showered down. It was a very hard climb. The queen tried climbing up another way, but she couldn't reach the opening in the rocks. Even Sylvia tried climbing up, and although she was very graceful, she wasn't good at climbing cliffs, and she had trouble keeping her balance among the shifting gravel and loose rocks.

And so the grown-ups tried helping each other. King Andrew climbed up a little way, then took hold of Paul's arm to pull him up. But Paul was very heavy and both men almost fell down together. Queen Jennifer tried boosting King Andrew from behind. Paul tried to help them both as best he could. It was very hard for everyone, but the king was able to help him climb up a little higher, nearly all the way up to the crack in the rock where Sylvia had pointed.

"I see it!" he cried. He was having a hard time staying up there. He struggled and strained. "There is one little marshmallow plant," said the king. "It's on the other side of the rocky crack! But the crack is too narrow! My arm is too big. I can't reach through!"

He tried and tried but he couldn't get his arm through the crack. Paul and Queen Jennifer couldn't hold him up any longer, and they all scrambled back down. All three of the grown-ups were now coated in dust. They were breathing hard and covered in little scratches from the sharp rocks.

"Maybe we can go around the hills and climb down from the other side," said Paul.

"No, the sun will be down soon," said the king.

"We'll lose our way and hurt ourselves in the dark."

"Let's ride back to the village," said Queen Jennifer. "We'll find some mountain climbers. They'll bring ropes and climbing gear. They can climb up there and get the marshmallow root."

"There's no time," said King Andrew. "We wouldn't reach the village until morning. Then we'd have to come back here, get the marshmallow root, and return late tomorrow night or maybe even the morning after that. Poor Sparkles can't wait that long."

"It's hopeless," said Queen Jennifer.

The king said, "If only we had a person who was small, good at climbing, and not afraid of heights."

"Me!" said Princess Juniper. "That's me!"

No one seemed to hear what she said.

"We're just not that good at climbing," said Paul. "And we're so big and heavy, we keep slipping and sliding on the loose rock."

"I can do it!" said Juniper. "Let me try!"

But no one listened to her.

"And even if we could get up there," said the queen, "how could we reach it? That crack is so narrow."

"Me! Me! Meee!" cried Juniper.

Finally, everyone turned to look at the little girl.

"Juniper, sweetheart," said King Andrew, "what are you shouting about? Can't you see that your mother and Paul and I are trying to think?"

"Wait," said the queen. "What about *Juniper?* She's light as a feather and all day long she does nothing but climb just like a tree frog. And her arms are small enough to reach the marshmallow plant!"

"That's what I've been trying to *tell* you!" Juniper hollered.

"Of course!" said the king. "I'm sorry, my dear. Yes! You're perfect for the job!"

## Chapter Eight

### SMALL ENOUGH TO MAKE A DIFFERENCE

THIS PART OF THE STORY ISN'T VERY INTERESTING.

You see, Princess Juniper didn't fall or struggle or fail. In other stories, when someone must make a dangerous climb, sometimes they slip or lose their grip, and they might even fall down and hurt themselves.

But not in this story.

In this story, Juniper didn't have any close calls, and she didn't slip. Not even a little bit. Instead, she walked up to the cliff and began to climb. As she hopped from one rock to another, getting higher and higher, she seemed very calm. She seemed to be having fun! She seemed very much, as her mother said, like a tree frog.

King Andrew cupped his hands around his mouth and called up to her. "Juniper, my dear, can you see the crack in the rock?"

"Yes," said Juniper. "I think so. It's just up above me." She hopped up a little farther.

"Juniper, my sweet child," shouted the queen, "are you quite all right? You won't fall, will you?"

"No," said Juniper. She lifted herself up to a higher boulder. "This is super easy."

"You're doing great," Paul shouted. "Don't be afraid!"

"I'm not," replied Juniper.

"Yip! Yip!" cried Sylvia.

Princess Juniper scrambled up a little more, and that was it. She had reached the rocky crack, and she saw the marshmallow plant, with its sugary sweet odor and its sugary white flower.

"I see it!" Juniper yelled down. "It's here!"

"She did it!" cried the king and queen and Paul together.

Sylvia wagged her tail.

Not only could Princess Juniper reach through the crack to grab the one marshmallow plant growing there, but she was able to squeeze all the way through the crack, where she found many other marshmallow plants. She gathered them gently, being sure to get all the roots. Then she placed them carefully in her pocket, squeezed out of the rocky crack, and climbed back down.

Everyone clapped and cheered as Princess Juniper held the plants up triumphantly.

"You did it!" said the queen, giving Juniper a big hug. "Thank goodness we had someone small with us. Now we can help Sparkles get well."

All at once, Juniper began to think about something that you are probably already thinking about. Earlier that day, Juniper had been worried about growing big and tall. But now she was very glad she was still *small.* If Juniper had been tall or big like Paul and her parents, there would have been no one to collect the marshmallow root. If she'd been big and tall, Sparkles would have to wait for the marshmallow root, and he might have gotten much more ill.

"Let's go home and save Sparkles!" she said.

The group got back on the unicorns and raced back to the castle stables.

When they got back to the castle, it was very late in the night. They found Sparkles lying in some hay with his eyes shut and breathing heavily. He didn't look well at all. Olivia and the doctor were by Sparkle's side. They stood up when they saw Juniper and the others.

"You got the marshmallow root!" said Olivia.

"Thanks to Juniper," said the queen. "It was growing on a high cliff behind some rocks. None of us could get to it in time. Only Juniper was small enough to make a difference."

Princess Juniper broke off some of the marshmallow root and held it close to Sparkles' nose.

Sparkles sniffed at it and then slowly opened his eyes. He nibbled just a little of the root from Princess Juniper's hand. Then he went back to sleep.

"Will he get better now?" Princess Olivia asked.

"I hope so," said the doctor. But we must wait for the medicine to work. Let's get some sleep and check on Sparkles in the morning."

## Chapter Nine

### A FULL RECOVERY

BEFORE GETTING DRESSED, BEFORE HAVING BREAKFAST, before doing anything else, the two princesses raced down to the castle stables as soon as they were awake so they could check on Sparkles.

But to their surprise, Sparkles wasn't in the stables.

"Where is he?" Princess Juniper asked.

"Let's check outside," said Princess Olivia.

Still wearing their nightgowns and slippers, they raced outside to see Sparkles prancing in the garden. Seeing the girls, Sparkles reared up and neighed happily. His black coat shone in the morning sun and his mane and tail sparkled in the breeze.

"He's all better!" Princess Juniper said.

"Good job, Sis," said Princess Olivia. "Hey, aren't you glad none of your crazy plans made you bigger?"

Princess Juniper blushed and nodded. "I guess I can wait a couple years to be tall," she said.

Just then, the king and queen arrived and were amazed to see how Sparkles had recovered.

Princess Olivia turned to her mom and dad. "I have an idea," she said. "Now that Sparkles is feeling better, can Juniper and I ride him together?"

"Both of us?" Princess Juniper asked. She smiled and her eyes shone. "At the same time?"

"Sparkles," said the queen, "how does that sound to you?"

The beautiful black unicorn stamped the grass and nodded his head.

"I think that's a yes," said Princess Olivia.

Princess Juniper hugged her sister. "Oh, riding with you is even better than getting to ride by myself."

The king saddled Sparkles and put on his harness. Sparkles knelt down so the girls could get on his back, and then they took off, riding through the crisp morning air and into the beauty of Wildflower Kingdom. The wildflowers were opening to greet the rising sun, and the meadow was dotted with purple, red, yellow, and orange.

As Princess Juniper sat in the saddle in front of Princess Olivia, she knew that someday she would grow as tall and strong as her older sister, but for now, she was happy being just the way she was.

# PLEASE LEAVE A REVIEW

Thank you for reading this book. We hope you enjoyed it! We would really appreciate it if you would please take a moment to review *The Princess and the Unicorn* on Amazon, Goodreads, or other retail sites. Thank you!

**WWW.AMLUZZADER.COM**

- blog
- freebies
- newsletter
- contact info

## About the Author

A.M. Luzzader is an award-winning children's author who writes chapter books and middle grade books. She specializes in writing books for preteens. A.M.'s fantasy adventure series 'A Mermaid in Middle Grade' is a magical coming of age book series for ages 8-12. She is also the author of the 'Hannah Saves the

World' series, which is a children's mystery adventure, also for ages 8-12.

A.M. decided she wanted to write fun stories for kids when she was still a kid herself. By the time she was in fourth grade, she was already writing short stories. In fifth grade, she bought a typewriter at a garage sale to put her words into print, and in sixth grade she added illustrations. Now that she has decided what she wants to be when she grows up, A.M. writes books for girls and boys full time. She was selected as the Writer of the Year in 2019-2020 by the League of Utah Writers.

A.M. is the mother of a 10-year-old and a 13-year-old who often inspire her stories. She lives with her husband and children in northern Utah. She is a devout cat person and avid reader.

A.M. Luzzader's books are appropriate for ages 5-12. Her chapter books are intended for kindergarten to third grade, and her middle grade books are for third grade through sixth grade. Find out more about A.M., sign up to receive her newsletter, and get special offers at her website: www.amluzzader.com.

facebook.com/a.m.luzzader

amazon.com/author/amluzzader

## About the Illustrator

Anna M. Clark is an artist who loves to draw, tell stories, and buy journals. She has worked as a baker, a math tutor, a security guard, an art teacher, and works now as an illustrator and artist!

She has traveled through Southeast Asia, was born on Halloween (the best holiday ever), and loves to create large chalk art murals. Anna lives with her husband in their cute apartment in Logan, Utah, with their beautiful basil plant.

Explore more of Anna M. Clark's work and her current projects at her website: annamclarkart.com.

OTHER BOOKS BY

# A.M. Luzzader

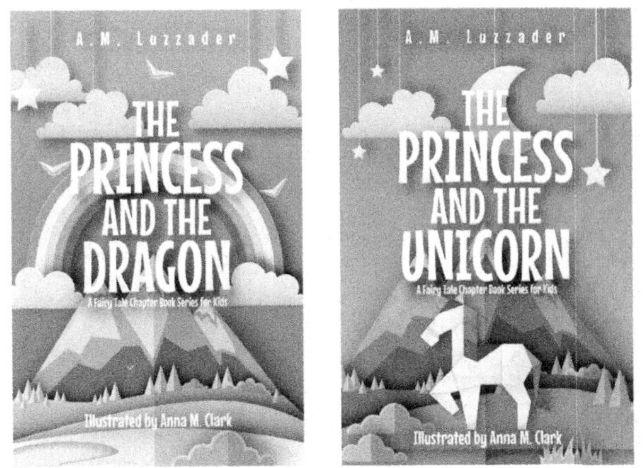


A Fairy Tale Chapter Book Series for Kids

For ages 6-8

OTHER BOOKS BY

# A.M. Luzzader

A Magic School for Girls
Chapter Book

For ages
6-8

OTHER BOOKS BY

# A.M. Luzzader

A Mermaid in Middle Grade
Books 1-3

For ages
8-12

# OTHER BOOKS BY

# A.M. Luzzader

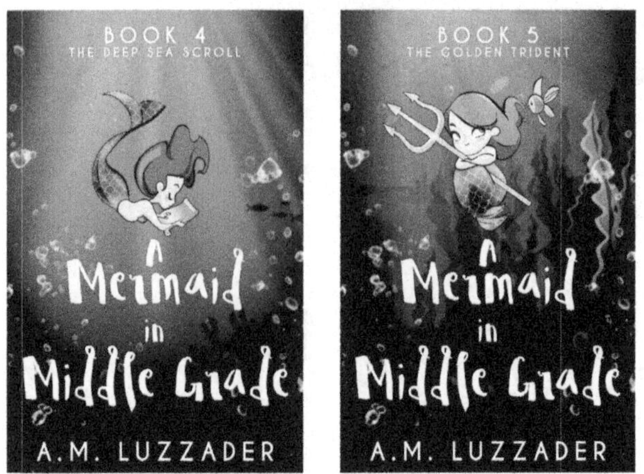


A Mermaid in Middle Grade
Books 4-6

For ages
8-12

OTHER BOOKS BY

# A.M. Luzzader

Hannah Saves the World
Books 1-3

For ages
8-12

OTHER BOOKS BY

# A.M. Luzzader

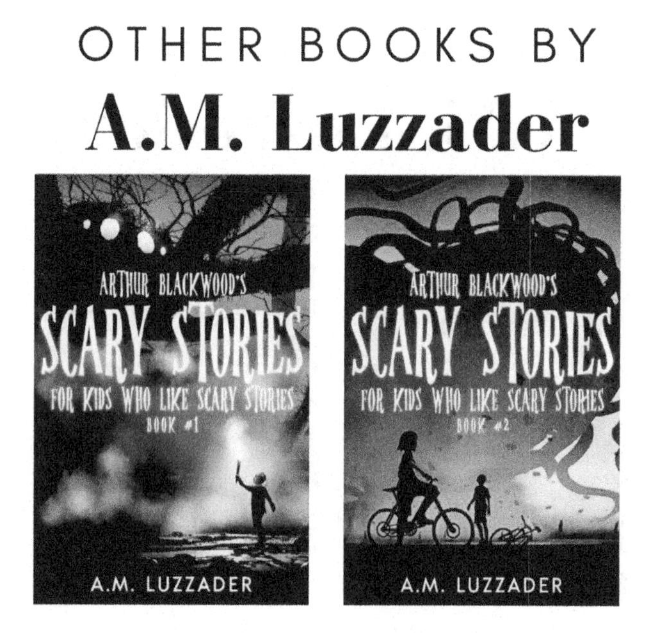


Arthur Blackwood's Scary Stories for Kids Who Like Scary Stories

Releasing 2021-2022

For ages 8-12